To Gina and Stephanie—
the original princesses
—J. R.

To Charles, who has turned
so many boxes into castles
—G. L.

Text copyright © 2012 by Jean Reidy
Illustrations copyright © 2012 by Geneviève Leloup

First published in the United States of America in January 2012
by Bloomsbury Books for Young Readers
www.bloomsburykids.com

For information about permission to reproduce selections from this book, write to
Permissions, Bloomsbury BFYR, 175 Fifth Avenue, New York, New York 10010

Library of Congress Cataloging-in-Publication Data
Reidy, Jean.
Too princessy! / by Jean Reidy ; illustrated by Geneviève Leloup. — 1st U.S. ed.
p.   cm.
Summary: A child rejects a number of playtime activities before settling on one that is just right.
ISBN 978-1-59990-722-2 (hardcover) • ISBN 978-1-59990-761-1 (reinforced)
[1. Stories in rhyme. 2. Play—Fiction. 3. Choice—Fiction.] I. Leloup, Geneviève, ill. II. Title.
PZ8.3.R2676Tnp 2012   [E]—dc23   2011025029

Art created in Adobe Illustrator
Typeset in Keener
Book design by Geneviève Leloup

Printed in China by C&C Offset Printing Co., Ltd., Shenzhen, Guangdong
4 6 8 10 9 7 5 3 (hardcover)
2 4 6 8 10 9 7 5 3 1 (reinforced)

FSC
www.fsc.org
MIX
Paper from
responsible sources
FSC® C008047

TOO PRINCESSY!

JEAN REIDY

ILLUSTRATED BY

GENEVIÈVE LELOUP

BLOOMSBURY

NEW YORK   LONDON   NEW DELHI   SYDNEY

I AM BORED!

TOO BLINKY,

TOO PLINKY.

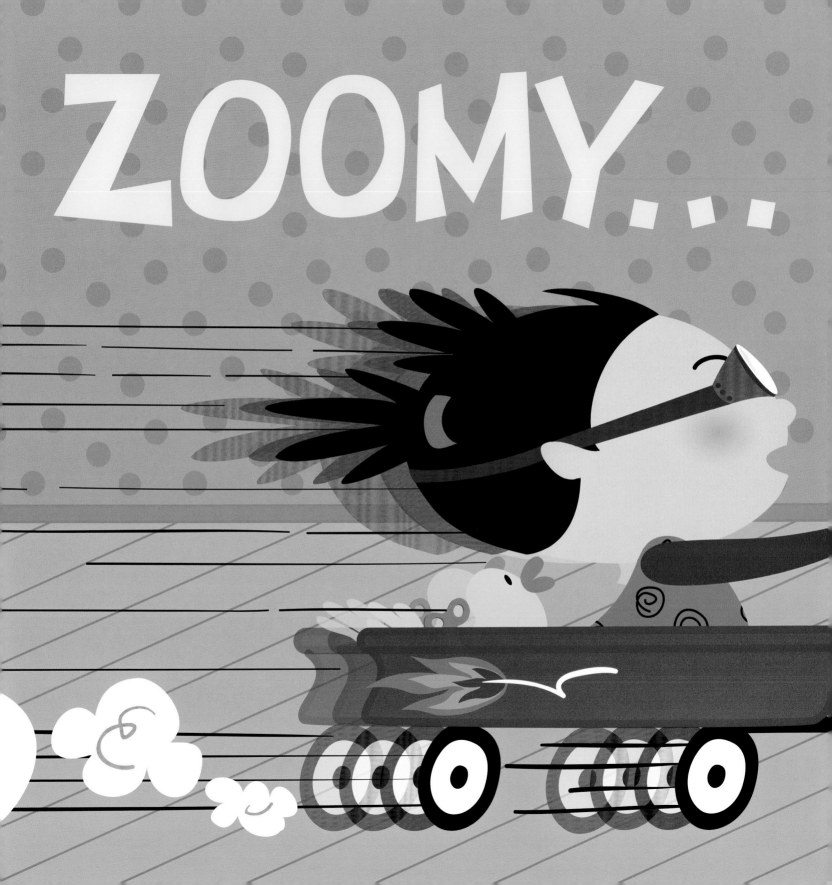

TOO PRINCESSY!

TOO CROWNY.

Once upon a time, **Jean Reidy** was a princess . . . as well as an Olympic figure skater, an astronaut, a rock-and-roll star, and a dreamer. She's still a dreamer. She writes from her home in Greenwood Village, Colorado, where she lives with her husband, Mike. Her four children and hordes of nieces and nephews provide her endless inspiration. Please visit her at www.jeanreidy.com.

Geneviève Leloup studied graphic arts, animation, and printing in Belgium, where she was born. Her whimsical illustrations have appeared in magazines and on various products, including lots of textiles and children's clothing. When not drawing or traveling, she bakes large amounts of cookies and plays accordion in her Brooklyn digs. You can visit her at www.alulustudio.com.